# Contents

# Scottish Summer Stories

with a foreword
by
Joan Lingard

Scottish **Book** Trust

THE SCOTSMAN
WRITING WORTH READING

Published by Scottish Book Trust
especially for *The Scotsman* in 2007

Scottish Book Trust
Sandeman House, Trunk's Close
55 High Street, Edinburgh EH1 1SR

www.scottishbooktrust.com
www.braw.org.uk

A CIP catalogue record for this book is available from the British Library

ISBN 978-1901077247

Designed and typeset by Lorraine McCallum

Commissioned with the support of the Scottish Arts Council

Scottish
**Arts** Council

Published and distributed in association with *The Scotsman*

THE SCOTSMAN
WRITING WORTH READING

Printed and bound in Great Britain by Nørhaven Paperback A/S

## Foreword by Joan Lingard

As Scottish Book Trust's children's patron, I am delighted to introduce this collection of new stories from 5 of Scotland's most talented writers for children. There are stories here for differing tastes and every age-group.

For younger readers we have tales of Mairi Hedderwick's Katie Morag and Aileen Paterson's Maisie, both highly treasured institutions, well-known and loved by millions of children over the years. Katie Morag on her idyllic Hebridean island finds a motherless baby seal and goes to his rescue while Maisie once again shows herself to be a streetwise Edinburgh cat. Girls who love princesses and are addicts of the popular Tiara Club will find a story about Princess Megan and a summer surprise, which she reveals in a letter to her friend Princess Amy. Alexander McCall Smith takes us forward to the summer of 2084 and the prospect of football being banned on the grounds that it is dangerous to health!

Then, for 10-14-year-olds, there is an amusing story from Catherine MacPhail involving a statue of St Ambrose and an elusive lottery ticket bearing a complete series of winning numbers.

Happy summer reading!

Joan Lingard

# Maisie Makes a Discovery!

a story for 6-8-year-olds

written and illustrated
by
Aileen Paterson

## Maisie Makes a Discovery!

Maisie Mackenzie is a tabby kitten with a fluffy coat of many colours. Orange and brown and black and white. She lives in Edinburgh, the capital of Scotland, and she wears a kilt. She has a granny and a daddy, and their home is a flat at the very top of a tall building. Next door lives pernickety, panloaf Mrs McKitty, who is a bit of a bossy boots. She doesn't like wild and woolly kittens who drop sweetie papers on the stairs, and make a lot of noise, and get up to mischief. Maisie and her best friend, Archie, have to mind their Ps and Qs when Mrs McKitty is about!

Although Maisie's home is in Edinburgh, she is a much-travelled kitten. Her daddy is a fearless explorer and sometimes he takes Maisie with him on his journeys to faraway places. She's been to Japan, and New York in America, and the island of Ballyhoo, where she was chased by naughty pirates. She's lived in a tree-house in the rainforest, and she found The Abominable Snowcat in Tibet. She's even been all the way to Glasgow on the train! She likes exploring and discovering things, just like Daddy. Her granny prefers peace and quiet, and Mrs McKitty thinks Maisie's daddy should get a nice job in the Morningside Bank.

Most of the time, Maisie goes to school and does her homework, like her friends. After school she plays with Archie, and they go exploring and discovering in the back green – except when Mrs McKitty has washing on the line. But, not long ago, Maisie made a very interesting discovery, in her own back green, in Morningside, at the beginning of the summer!

It's easy to tell when summer has arrived in Edinburgh. All of a sudden the sun shines all day and the sky is a cloudless blue. All the cats in all the flats open their windows wide to let the fresh air in, and kittens stop wearing vests. The nippy east wind has turned into a warm gentle breeze.

## Maisie Makes a Discovery!

In Morningside Mansions, where Maisie lives, summer began one Saturday morning. She could tell right away. Mrs McKitty had taken the 23 bus to Princes Street, wearing an enormous flowery hat. And, my word, when she and Granny went shopping in Morningside Road, she was allowed to wear a T-shirt, and MY goodness, Granny wasn't wearing a coat! She'd put on a nice cosy cardigan instead. It was a lovely day, and everyone looked cheerful and happy.

When they returned home, Granny put the groceries away and began making sandwiches for lunch. While Granny got busy, Maisie went into the sitting room and looked out of the window. There were lots of birds about. The arrival of summer had made them cheerful and chirpy too. A blackbird was whistling from his perch on top of the shed, and 16 starlings were swinging on the clothesline. High in the sky a flock of seagulls was wheeling round and round, and a black and white magpie was flying in and out of the big tree at the bottom of the back green, where he had a nest.

Like all cats and kittens, Maisie enjoyed bird-watching. She'd read Daddy's books about them, and she thought they were very interesting. Unlike kittens, they enjoyed eating worms and beetles, and some of them could whistle, and, of course, they could FLY.

She leaned on the windowsill and gave a happy sigh. There was nowhere nicer than home, sweet home, on a peaceful summery Saturday.

Suddenly, the peace of Morningside was shattered!

Terrible yowlings and growlings filled the air!

All the birds flew off as fast as their wings could carry them!

Maisie nearly jumped out of her skin!

WHAT COULD IT BE?

Heads began popping out of all the open windows nearby. One of the heads was a ginger one. It belonged to her friend, Archie. He waved to her, then disappeared. She ran off to find Granny, who was just as puzzled and alarmed as she was. Next minute...the yowls grew nearer and nearer...they held their breath...then Mrs McKitty rushed through the kitchen door...still YOWLING.

Granny was flabbergasted.

"Dearie me, Marjorie," she cried. "What's the matter? What's caused all the kerfuffle?"

"Kerfuffle indeed! I've been robbed. Robbed! In broad daylight! Some hooligan climbed into my bedroom while I was out, and STOLE my precious diamond brooch. It was on the table by the window. We must phone for the police, Isabella.

I'm shattered to fragments. Morningside is going to POT."

Granny ran to the telephone, looking worried. Nothing like this had ever happened before.

Maisie put on the kettle.

Soon, two policecats arrived, followed by Archie, who was keen to get the news from Maisie. The policecats, Sergeant MacStooshie and Constable Clawford, began to investigate. They asked lots of questions and examined the table where the missing brooch had been, and the windowsill. Then, followed by Mrs McKitty, Granny, Maisie and Archie, they went downstairs and out of the back door, and onto the back green.

## Maisie Makes a Discovery!

Heads popped out of windows again when the local cats realised the policecats were on the prowl. Unfortunately, no one had seen any strangers getting up to no good.

"Gosh, Maisie," whispered Archie, "isn't this exciting? A REAL crime, right here on our doorstep. When I grow up, I want to be a detective, on the trail of cat burglars."

"SHOOSH!" cried Mrs McKitty. "Little kittens should be seen and not heard."

"SHOOSH! The lot of you!" growled Sergeant MacStooshie. "And keep off the grass. We're hunting for important clues."

After an hour of pussyfooting all over the back green, all that turned up was a clothes peg...

Sergeant MacStooshie sighed.

Next, the policecats turned their attention to a drainpipe which went all the way up the wall of the building, right up to the roof. It was black and shiny and it passed right next to Mrs McKitty's bedroom window. In the earth at the foot of the drainpipe there were several paw prints! A CLUE...AT LAST!

Sergeant MacStooshie smiled.

"There's no doubt about it, PC Clawford, these prints belong to our robber. He's clawed his way up this drainpipe and made off with the jewel. We'll soon trace him and put the pawcuffs on the scoundrel."

"That's great news, sir...but have you noticed how wee these paw prints are? I think we're looking for a kitten. I think we're looking for a kitten who lives nearby, and knew that Mrs McKitty was away down to Princes Street."

## Maisie Makes a Discovery!

"By Jove, you're right!"

Sergeant MacStooshie and Constable Clawford turned round and stared at...Maisie. They asked her to stand in the earth beside the robber's prints...her paw prints MATCHED PERFECTLY!

Granny gasped and took Maisie's paw. Mrs McKitty turned PURPLE.

"Well now, young Maisie, what have you been up to?" asked the sergeant.

"That's what I want to know!" cried Mrs McKitty. "What HAVE you been up to?"

Maisie's head was filled with thoughts of pawcuffs and police stations.

"I haven't been up to anything, not even a drainpipe!" she wailed.

Archie stepped forward.

"It's true," he cried. "Maisie's my best friend and she's not a robber. These are her paw prints. She was practising climbing yesterday, with me, but she couldn't climb up the drainpipe. It was too shiny and slippery. You can see, there's not a single scratch on it."

Sergeant MacStooshie checked. Archie was right, and Maisie wasn't in trouble, but the mystery remained. There were no clues, and he was hot and hungry.

He scratched his head...

"It's a puzzle. No cat burglar could have climbed up to the top floor without leaving a trace. It's just as if he'd flown up there."

Maisie's ears pricked up and she looked up at the sky. She remembered what she had seen that morning, and she wondered if she could solve the mystery...

With a loud MEOW, she raced across the grass and began to climb up the big old tree beside the wall. The others wondered what was going on.

Maisie climbed right up into the tree until she was hidden amongst the leaves. At last, she found what she was looking for – THE MAGPIE'S NEST. She'd remembered that in one of Daddy's books, she'd read that magpies sometimes steal shiny things for their nests...and, yes...it was true. She put her paw inside and lifted out the glittering brooch, then she jumped down to the ground.

"I'VE FOUND IT!"

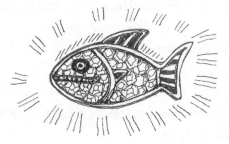

"You are a credit to Morningside. I've always said so," purred Mrs McKitty, pinning the brooch on her blouse.

"You're a clever wee scone," said Granny, giving her a cuddle.

"Well done!" said Sergeant MacStooshie. "You and Archie are both grand young detectives, so you are."

All the cats watching from the windows cheered!

To celebrate the great discovery, everyone went up to Granny's flat for salmon sandwiches and strawberry tarts, even Sergeant MacStooshie and PC Clawford.

Afterwards, Granny had a wee nap and Maisie and Archie had a game of football. The birds came out to watch, all except the magpie – who sat on top of a clothes pole, chattering crossly. Mrs McKitty went home and shut her windows. (She didn't want any more BIRD burglars in her bedroom!)

The sun was shining, and everybody was cheerful and happy again, but they would never forget the day that summer arrived in Edinburgh.

TOOTALOOTHENOO!

## More Maisie titles to enjoy:

| | |
|---|---|
| Maisie and the Botanic Garden Mystery<br>*(available from the Edinburgh Botanic Gardens Shop)* | ISBN: 187229135X |
| Maisie and the Abominable Snowcat | ISBN: 1871512794 |
| Maisie Bites the Big Apple | ISBN: 1871512697 |
| Maisie Digs up the Past | ISBN: 1871512417 |
| Maisie Goes to a Wedding | ISBN: 1871512549 |
| Maisie Goes to Hollywood | ISBN: 1871512409 |
| Maisie Goes to Hospital | ISBN: 1871512069 |
| Maisie Goes to School | ISBN: 1871512018 |
| Maisie in the Rainforest | ISBN: 1871512298 |
| Maisie Jumps into Japan | ISBN: 1871512654 |
| Maisie Loves Paris | ISBN: 1871512050 |
| Maisie and the Pirates | ISBN: 1871512557 |
| Maisie and the Posties | ISBN: 1871512034 |
| Maisie's Festival Adventure | ISBN: 1871512042 |
| Maisie's Merry Christmas | ISBN: 1871512468 |
| Maisie and the Puffer | ISBN: 1871512336 |
| Meusaidh anns a' Choille-Uisge | ISBN: 1871512484 |
| Meusaidh anns an Sgoil | ISBN: 1871512476 |
| What Maisie Did Next | ISBN: 1871512093 |

**Find out more about Aileen Paterson and view a complete list of her children's books at www.braw.org.uk.**

# The Tiara Club

# Princess Megan and the Summer Surprise

a story for 6-8-year-olds

by
Vivian French

*Letters from her Royal Highness Princess Megan to Princess Amy, her dear friend from The Royal Palace Academy for the Preparation of Perfect Princesses. (Known to all students as The Princess Academy.)*

## Princess Megan and the Summer Surprise

Dear Amy

Isn't it weird? I thought the school summer holidays would be SO fabulous – but guess what? I'm BORED! I miss you and everyone else at school dreadfully. The Princess Academy is such fun! Although I don't think they'll ever manage to turn me into a Perfect Princess, however hard they try. Can you imagine you and me and Alice and all the others being ABSOLUTELY PERFECT PRINCESSES every minute of every day? I can't!

Mum and Dad are on tour again, and Grandmother does her best, but she has a little sleep after breakfast and then another in the afternoon and there's nothing for me to do. I've done ALL my holiday homework already – that'll show you just how bored I am. I've been practising Sweeping Curtsies When Holding a Full Cup of Tea every single day; you wouldn't believe how good I've got! If Queen Mother Matilda doesn't give me at least 10 tiara points next term I'll be really disappointed.

Please, PLEASE write soon and tell me everything you've been doing...

Lots and lots of love
Megan

Dear Amy

You're SO lucky! Fancy meeting up with Charlotte and Alice and Olivia at the Royal Exhibition! I hope you told them I was missing them. The only news here is that I left a skipping rope in the throne room (I did mean to tidy it up) and the prime minister tripped over it and Grandmother was furious. Oh, and she found all the cups I'd broken before I got good at Sweeping Curtsies, and she wasn't very pleased about that either. Still, at least she's decided I need something to do. She's been asked to visit a school friend she hasn't seen for years and YEARS, and she says she'll take me with her if I promise to be good. I'm being ANGELIC. Anything's better than walking round balancing cups of tea.

Lots of love
Megan

PS What did you mean when you said something nice might happen?

## Princess Megan and the Summer Surprise

Dear lovely wonderful Amy

Wow, wow, WOW! Do you mean it? Me? Come to your birthday party? A Princess Sleepover? That is SO wonderful! I'm writing very quickly to say YES and thank you a million billion times. And please thank your mother and father too. Are you asking all the Rose and Poppy Room princesses? I absolutely can't wait – it'll be SUCH fun. Thank you again and again.

Megan x x x

PS I haven't actually asked Grandmother yet but I'm sure she'll say I can come.

Dear Amy

I want to die. Grandmother says I've got to go with her to visit her friend because we accepted that invitation first. She says Perfect Princesses always keep their word. Please give my love to everyone and say I'm very, VERY sorry not to be at the party.

Megan

PS Have a LOVELY birthday. I'm sorry I've smudged the ink. I can't help crying.

Dear Amy

Grandmother's still cross. I couldn't help blowing my nose and sniffing all the way to her friend's house, and she said I was a silly girl and she was ashamed of me. I don't think her friend noticed I'd been crying, though. Her name's Queen Frizella Marie, and she looks about a thousand years old with whiskers on her chin, and she's got 3 yappy dogs. And I know a Perfect Princess should never make nasty remarks, but I do think she's rude. She gave a kind of shrug when Grandmother introduced me, and said, "My sweet precious girlies are arriving later today. I suppose you can play with them." Grandmother looked very surprised, but she didn't ask who Queen Frizella meant. Maybe it's more dogs?

Lots of love
Megan

Amy!

You'll NEVER guess what's happened! THE HORRIBLE TWINS ARE HERE! It turns out Queen Frizella Marie is their great-aunt. When they climbed out of their carriage I nearly fell over backwards with surprise. Queen Frizella introduced them to Grandmother, and then pointed at me and said, "She's here too, my darling popsy posies. You don't have to play with her unless you want to."

Diamonde gave me the coldest stare. "Oh! It's Megan! I thought your funny little palace was miles and miles away."

I didn't know WHAT to say. Luckily Grandmother had closed her eyes for a moment, and I don't think she heard. Then Gruella, who was actually looking a bit uncomfortable, suggested we took the dogs for a walk, and that's what we did. Diamonde wouldn't come. She said she wanted to unpack.

"Remember this is MY great-aunt's house," she told me when we got back. "Great-Auntie Friz told me she didn't even ask you. She only asked your grandmother, but your grandmother begged and begged her to let you come and Auntie Friz didn't like to say no." And then she made a face. "Your grandmother's very doddery, isn't she? She keeps going to sleep."

Honestly, Amy – she was so awful I lost my temper. It was bad enough her being snooty to me, but my gran is lovely even if she does sleep a lot.

"Actually," I snapped, "Amy asked me to her birthday party, but Grandmother had already made an arrangement with your great-aunt, and it would have been rude not to come."

Diamonde snorted. "Don't tell fibs. If Amy was having a birthday party she'd have invited me and Gruella. She likes us MUCH better than you. Doesn't she, Gruella?" Before Gruella could answer Queen Frizella's butler beat a loud Boing! Boing! on a gong.

"Tea's ready," Gruella said, and she hurried me and Diamonde downstairs.

I thought it would be just us and the queen and Grandmother, but a very ancient-looking king had joined them in the grand withdrawing room.

"May I present my delightful little great-nieces, the Perfect Princesses Diamonde and Gruella, King Sebastian," Queen Frizella Marie said as we walked in. "Oh, and my friend's granddaughter... what's your name, child?"

It was SO weird! Grandmother suddenly sat bolt upright, and said in the CHILLIEST voice,

"Her name is Princess Megan, Frizella." And she turned and gave me a lovely smile as I curtsied to the king.

"Megan." Queen Frizella nodded. "Well, perhaps Megan could help my darling twins with the tea? A Perfect Princess should always be willing to serve those more important than herself."

"That's right, Auntie." Diamonde put her head on one side, and gave her great-aunt a sickly sweet smile. "I'll pour the tea, and Megan can hand it round. Gruella, you can do the sugar."

"SUCH a precious princess." Queen Frizella Marie beamed back at Diamonde, and Diamonde began to pour tea from the silver teapot.

Can you guess what she did? I bet you can! She filled the first cup absolutely to the brim.

"Here you are, Megan," she sneered. "And DO try not to spill any! My great-aunt's rose petal tea is famous, and we don't want any wasted."

I saw my grandmother's face – and she was FURIOUS! She was absolutely glaring at Diamonde, and the king was staring as well.

I stood up quickly. "I'll do my best," I said, and I took the cup and walked steadily towards King Sebastian. I swept into my deepest curtsey – and I didn't spill a drop! But as the king took the tea from me his hand shook – and rose petal tea slopped into the saucer.

"See? I knew Megan would spill it!" Diamonde said spitefully.

The old king frowned at her. "But the cup was much too full!" He patted my arm. "You did very well, Princess Megan. Very well indeed. Only a truly Perfect Princess could have held the cup so steadily. You must have worked very hard at your deportment lessons." He paused, and gave Diamonde a cold stare. "Perhaps you go to school elsewhere, my dear?"

"The teapot was too heavy," Diamonde said crossly. "Besides, I can do just as well as Megan. Better!" She seized the teapot, and poured another cup – and I couldn't help noticing it wasn't nearly as full as the last one. She picked it up and walked towards my grandmother, sank into a curtsey – and the cup slipped off the saucer. It crashed to the floor, and the tea went EVERYWHERE! Grandmother's skirt was soaked, and she jumped up with a shriek.

Diamonde screamed as well, and Queen Frizella Marie rushed to her side. "Are you burnt, my poor baby? Where does it hurt? Quick! Show your auntie."

And then – oh, Amy! I DO wish you'd been there to see for yourself. Grandmother stepped forward, and her back was as straight as a ramrod. "Frizella Marie," she said in the most SQUASHING sort of voice, "you were a silly girl when you were at school, and you're a silly woman now. I hoped you had changed, but you haven't. I made a mistake coming here, and I made a worse mistake when I insisted that my granddaughter came with me. I should have realised what a treasure she is, and allowed her to spend time with her own friends." She swirled round, and beckoned to a footman. "My carriage, if you please, young man. If we're quick, Megan will be just in time for Princess Amy's sleepover party!"

So that was the end of our visit, and I'm sending this with the messenger who's galloping on ahead to say I'm on my way! I just HAD to tell you what happened.

I can't WAIT to see you and everybody.

LOTS of love
Megan x x x

PS King Sebastian left when we did, and do you know what he said to Grandmother? He said, "No wonder those twins are so foolish. Just look at their relations!"

# The Tiara Club

Princess Charlotte and
  the Birthday Ball                  ISBN: 978 1 84362 863 7

Princess Katie and
  the Silver Pony                    ISBN: 978 1 84362 860 6

Princess Daisy and
  the Dazzling Dragon                ISBN: 978 1 84362 864 4

Princess Alice and
  the Magical Mirror                 ISBN: 978 1 84362 861 3

Princess Sophia and
  the Sparkling Surprise             ISBN: 978 1 84362 862 0

Princess Emily and
  the Beautiful Fairy                ISBN: 978 1 84362 859 0

# The Tiara Club at Silver Towers

Princess Charlotte and
  the Enchanted Rose                 ISBN: 978 1 84616 195 7

Princess Katie and
  the Dancing Broom                  ISBN: 978 1 84616 196 4

Princess Daisy and the
  Magical Merry-Go-Round             ISBN: 978 1 84616 197 1

Princess Alice and
  the Crystal Slipper                ISBN: 978 1 84616 198 8

Princess Sophia and
  the Prince's Party                 ISBN: 978 1 84616 199 5

Princess Emily and
  the Wishing Star                   ISBN: 978 1 84616 200 8

## The Tiara Club at Ruby Mansions

| | |
|---|---|
| Princess Chloe and the Primrose Petticoats | ISBN: 978 1 84616 290 9 |
| Princess Jessica and the Best-Friend Bracelet | ISBN: 978 1 84616 291 6 |
| Princess Georgia and the Shimmering Pearl | ISBN: 978 1 84616 292 3 |
| Princess Olivia and the Velvet Cloak | ISBN: 978 1 84616 293 0 |
| Princess Lauren and the Diamond Necklace | ISBN: 978 1 84616 294 7 |
| Princess Amy and the Golden Coach | ISBN: 978 1 84616 295 4 |
| Christmas Wonderland | ISBN: 978 1 84616 296 1 |
| Butterfly Ball | ISBN: 978 1 84616 470 5 |

All priced at £3.99. Christmas Wonderland and Butterfly Ball are priced at £5.99. The Tiara Club books are available from all good bookshops, or can be ordered direct from the publisher:

Orchard Books, PO BOX 29, Douglas IM99 1BQ.

For credit card orders please telephone 01624 836000 or fax 01624 837033, visit our website: www.wattspub.co.uk or e-mail: bookshop@enterprise.net for details.

To order please quote title, author and ISBN and your full name and address.

Cheques and postal orders should be made payable to "Bookpost Plc".

Postage and packing is FREE within the UK (overseas customers should add £2.00 per book).

Prices and availability are subject to change.

**Find out more about Vivian French and view a complete list of her children's books at www.braw.org.uk.**

# Katie Morag: Summer Visitors and the Tiresome Ted Sea Shanties

a story and poems for 8-10-year-olds,
with an exclusive new afterword and artwork

written and illustrated
by
Mairi Hedderwick

## Summer Visitors

Many visitors come on holiday to the island in the summer. Katie Morag's mother and father are forever emptying boxes and stacking shelves, polishing the counter and fussing around the Holiday People. Katie Morag gets very bored.

One summer, Mrs McColl decided to make a fancy arrangement in the shop window for the visitors to admire.

"Go down to the shore, Katie Morag, for some sand and seaweed. Just to add the finishing touch," said Mrs McColl as she stacked a pyramid of beach balls under an archway of buckets and spades. "And anything else that would look good," she added.

Katie Morag shovelled a layer of sand and then a layer of seaweed into her bogie. She scanned the tide line. Further along the shore there was something strange. Dark and shiny, it looked like a wet rumpled jacket; but it was moving. The sleeve bit was waving at her. Katie Morag was more interested than frightened. What could have been buttons seemed more like eyes and, sure enough, when Katie Morag got closer, the buttons blinked.

"A baby seal!" cried Katie Morag. She looked out to sea. The mother must be hunting for fish in the bay. Katie Morag looked long and hard. But no head bobbed up out of the waves to check all was well with the pup.

The seal pup stared at Katie Morag with large appealing eyes.

You would look very good in the seaside display! thought Katie Morag. Suddenly the shop was an exciting place to be. "I'll look after you," said Katie Morag. "I'll call you Ròn."

"Take that seal back where he belongs!" exclaimed Mrs McColl. "He is most definitely NOT going in my window display!"

Before she could say more, Ròn with a heave on his flippers, lurched from the bogie on to the window shelf. Buckets and spades and balls went in all directions.

Mrs McColl was furious.

Katie Morag raced down the brae to catch the bouncing balls and bumped into the Holiday Children. They said they would help her take the seal pup back.

Katie Morag had a heavy heart as she pushed Ròn down to the water's edge. He flippered away into the sea.

No mother came to meet him, within minutes he was back at Katie Morag's feet. She tried again to shove him off but the same thing happened again. Back he came! Her new friends cheered.

"We'll just have to look after you ourselves, then!" said Katie Morag, delighted with Ròn's return.

They sneaked him into the shed when no one was looking and got lots more seaweed for a bed. Mr McColl's barrel of salt herring was very convenient.

Feeding Ròn was difficult. He did not like the Ferryman's wife's chocolate cake but he scoffed left-over fish fingers from Katie Morag's tea, no bother at all. But Katie Morag didn't have fish fingers for tea every day. Soon the barrel of salt herring was empty.

"He eats an awful lot," said Jake.

"And he's not toilet trained," sniffed Jemma, "is he?"

"Well no…" agreed Katie Morag, wondering. Katie Morag was worried about the empty barrel but most worried about Ròn.

She and the Holiday Children tried dangling their fishing lines over the edge of the old pier but nobody caught anything.

"There are lots of fish in the sea," moaned Katie Morag, "but we are no good at catching them. I bet Ròn could though, if he really tried."

This time when Katie Morag pushed Ròn into the sea they all shouted and yelled when he came back. They banged bits of driftwood together and waved flags of torn netting. The seal looked a bit surprised but, eventually, he turned and headed out for the deep sea where the best fishes live.

Katie Morag was glad Ròn had gone home. She climbed slowly back up the brae to the shop and the Post Office.

"Can my friends come in for tea?" she asked.

"Of course!" said Mrs McColl.

"As long as they don't eat as much as Ròn..." smiled Mr McColl.

That night before she went to bed Katie Morag looked out of her window. She was sure she saw Ròn's head in the bay – or was it a beach ball?

# Afterword

*Summer Visitors* is based on an incident that happened when my children were young.

Our house was beside the sea. A wild summer storm one night saw us early on the beach next morning looking for driftwood.

Mark and Tammie spied the black object on the shore. The seal pup was thin and immobile; stranded on the tide line, no mother in sight. It looked appealingly at us but bared sharp teeth as we approached. We had to do something. We wrapped it in a seaweed-stuffed anorak and put it in a fish box in the byre. Feeding it with milk and cod liver oil from the pet lamb's bottle was not a success. It would not swallow.

Next day, distressed and reluctant, Mark and Tammie helped take Ròn back to the shore. There in the bay was his mother! We adults were sure of that. Ròn came alive at the water's edge, corkscrewing through the waves to meet up with her.

Mark and Tammie would often return to the beach to call his name. It was hard telling them that we had done the right thing.

# The Tiresome Ted Sea Shanties
# Katie Morag has Lost her Ted

Katie Morag has lost her Ted
And can't tell where to find him.
Leave him alone and he'll come home,
The wind and the tide behind him.

# Of All the Fish that Swim in the Sea

Of all the fish that swim in the sea,
The Tiresome Ted is the one for me.

A Herring's no use to cuddle in bed;
Cuddle a herring? I'd rather be dead!

Mackerels are slippery, most used for bait,
Some doused in vinegar, 6 to a plate.

Flounders are flatfish; that everyone knows,
But under the sand they nibble your toes.

Eels have got teeth, sharp set in their jaw.
Down deep a-snaking – is that what I saw?

The Cod is the King and that's no mistake,
But sooner or later he's just plain fishcake.

Of all the fish that swim in the sea,
The Tiresome Ted is the one for me.

# What Shall She Do?

What shall she do
With a soaking teddy
Washed up on the seashore?

Hang him on the washline
Till he's fluffy;
Wind and sun together.

Put him by the fireside
Till he's cosy;
In your Grannie's kitchen.

Feed him mince and tatties
Till he's pudgy;
Put him on his potty.

Brush his fur and comb him
Till he's lovely;
In the baby's nightie.

Sing a lullaby song
Till he's sleepy.
Then take him into bed.

## More books featuring Katie Morag, published by the Random House Group Ltd and available from all good bookshops:

| | |
|---|---|
| Katie Morag and the Grand Concert | ISBN: 978-0099262756 |
| Katie Morag and the New Pier | ISBN: 978-0099220824 |
| Katie Morag and the Riddles | ISBN: 978-0099414186 |
| Katie Morag and the Tiresome Ted | ISBN: 978-0099118817 |
| Katie Morag and the Two Grandmothers | ISBN: 978-0099118718 |
| Katie Morag and the Wedding | ISBN: 978-0099463412 |
| Katie Morag Delivers the Mail | ISBN: 978-0099220725 |
| Katie Morag of Course! | ISBN: 978-0099432050 |
| Katie Morag and the Dancing Class | ISBN: 978-0370329109 |
| Katie Morag's Island Stories | ISBN: 978-0099438564 |
| More Katie Morag Island Stories | ISBN: 978-0099433033 |
| The Big Katie Morag Storybook | ISBN: 978-0099720317 |
| The Second Katie Morag Storybook | ISBN: 978-0099264743 |

## Find out more about Mairi Hedderwick and view a complete list of her children's books at www.braw.org.uk.

# The Summer
# of 2084

a story for 8-10-year-olds

by
Alexander McCall Smith
illustrated by Brett Hudson

## The Summer of 2084

It was a nightmare, and when Jimmy first heard the news he could hardly believe it. What dreadful news to get just before the summer holidays!

"It can't be true," he said, his eyes wide with disbelief. "No football! It just can't be true."

But his friend Tom nodded. "It is," he said sadly. "I heard it on the news. Football is going to be banned, starting tomorrow."

Jimmy thought about this conversation as he made his way to school that day. Why, he wondered, would they ban football? He could think of no reason at all, and decided that perhaps Tom had misheard. Perhaps they had banned something else that sounded like football. Perhaps that was the explanation.

But Tom had been quite right, and that morning the whole school gathered in the hall to hear the news from the Head Teacher herself.

"As you may have heard," said the Head Teacher, casting a watchful eye over the rows of pupils, "football has been banned as from today. The First Ministress has made an announcement that in the interests of safety" – and she repeated the word to give it extra effect – "safety, it has been decided that football will no longer be played."

The boys looked at each other in astonishment. Ban football? The First Ministress had banned lots of things – skateboards, for example, and fish and chips and soor plooms – but football!

"You may be wondering," the Head Teacher went on, "why this has been done. Well, there is a very good reason. It's been clear for a very long time that football is a dangerous game. People run about, chasing after a ball, and that means that they might fall over. And if they fall over, they may graze their knees, or even sprain their ankles. We can't have that, can we?"

There was complete silence. Then one of the girls said, "No, we can't. It's about time they banned it."

Several other girls clapped their hands at this, and the Head Teacher smiled encouragingly. "Well, at least some people can see reason," she said. "And so here, boys and girls, here is a new sign that you'll be seeing over the next few days."

She turned to a poster which had been concealed by a white sheet and which she now uncovered with a flourish. And this is what it showed – a football with a line through the middle. Underneath it, in large letters, was the simple message: DANGEROUS!

With sinking hearts, the boys listened as the Head Teacher went on.

"In order to make sure that nobody plays this dangerous game," she said, "all boys who own a football will be required to bring it to school and have it locked away. And no cheating! There will be a heavy fine for any boy found hiding a football!"

At lunch that day, one of the dinner men leaned across and whispered into Jimmy's ear as he served him with his lettuce and carrots. "I've heard about this football business," he said. "It's bad luck for boys. But that's what it's like these days since the girls took over."

Jimmy was about to say something back to him, to tell him that there were some girls who actually liked football, but the dinner man put a finger to his lips in a gesture of silence. "Careful," the man whispered. "She's watching us."

He pointed in the direction of the Head Teacher, who was standing at the other end of the room, watching the children for any signs of dangerous behaviour. Jimmy shivered. It was all very strange.

The next morning the footballs were collected. Every boy in the school who owned a football had brought it in and handed it over to the janitor. Jimmy had brought the football that his parents had bought him for his last birthday, when he had turned 10. It was a very fine football, complete with a Hearts crest on it.

He loved that football and it broke his heart to hand it over and see it join the forlorn pile of other footballs that had been brought in.

It seemed to him so unfair that people should be stopped from doing the things they liked just because there was a very slight risk of something like a grazed knee or a sore ankle. Why, everything has a little bit of risk attached to it, and if we wrapped ourselves up in cotton wool we would end up doing nothing at all. Swimming had already been banned and school outings too. Now they could no longer play football, what was left? Very little, thought Jimmy. And he thought how dull the summer holidays would be if there was no football. What on earth would he do to pass the time?

And then a new boy came to the school, a boy from one of the islands in the north. His name was Magnus, and he had a wide smile and clear blue eyes that seemed to have a light shining in them. When you looked at Magnus, you thought for a moment that you were looking at the sun.

Jimmy found himself talking to Magnus at the end of the new boy's first day at school.

"There's something wrong with this place," said Magnus. "Everybody seems unhappy."

Jimmy nodded. "We are," he said. "We're very unhappy."

"Why?" asked Magnus. "Why are you unhappy?"

Jimmy looked at his new friend. Surely he knew. But perhaps not – he came from far away, and perhaps word of the First Ministress's decision had not reached that far. "It's because we aren't allowed to play football," he explained. "Football's banned now, you know. Even the big teams have been told to stop playing, in case they hurt themselves. Hearts has closed down. They've been told to take up ballet instead."

Magnus looked very surprised. "Ballet?"

"Yes," said Jimmy. "Apparently it's much safer. And the First Ministress prefers it."

Magnus was silent for a while. Then he spoke. "But that's nonsense!" he said. "Obviously people shouldn't do really dangerous things, but football is just fun.

Who minds a grazed knee or a sore ankle as long as you can have some fun?"

Jimmy thought that he was right, but when people decided that things were dangerous then there was not too much that you could do. As the Head Teacher had put it, "The Government really does know what's best for you and you really shouldn't argue. So keep quiet."

Magnus looked thoughtful. "I'm going to have a game of football," he burst out. "I don't care."

Jimmy drew in his breath. This was daring talk, and was in itself very, very dangerous. What if one of the girls saw Magnus playing football – she would almost certainly tell the Head Teacher, and then there would be dreadful trouble. Did Magnus not know that you couldn't argue with people who decided what was good for you? Where had he been living all this time not to know that?

Jimmy did not dare to mention to anybody else the conversation he had had with Magnus. The next day in class, in the middle of the sewing lesson, he looked across the room at Magnus and the other boy gave a little nod. Jimmy's heart leapt. Had he really brought a football to school? he asked himself.

He had. In the interval, when all the children were standing about in the playground – running was not allowed, of course, and even walking had to be done with permission – Jimmy saw Magnus come out of the classroom with something tucked under his jersey. And then, in a glorious moment, he pulled up his jersey and revealed a shining new football.

"Football!" Magnus shouted out. "Who wants a game of football?"

Several of the girls screamed. "You can't!" shouted one of them. "It's not allowed any more!"

Magnus glared at her. It seemed that his eyes were on fire. "Oh yes?" he said. "We'll see about that!"

And with that he tossed the ball high into the air and ran out to catch it as it fell. Jimmy looked about him, uncertain what to do. He was not one to break the rules, but when the rules were so stupid, then surely, you had the right to do something about it.

"I'll play," he shouted. "Kick it over to me, Magnus."

And with that, all the other boys ran forward and joined in. Soon they were having a wonderful game of football while the girls looked on in horror.

And then an extraordinary thing happened. A few men walking along the road outside the school saw what was happening and one of them dashed into a house and came out again holding a football which he had hidden away when the ban had come in. Soon the men were playing a game in the street, shouting with joy, as the boys were doing.

And so it spread throughout the city, and all across the country too. Everywhere, people discovered footballs that had been hidden away and began to play the game that had been so unkindly taken from them. And the professional players, the ones from Hearts, stripped off their ballet outfits and got back into their football kits. "We can play again," they shouted. "We can play!"

The First Ministress was furious, of course, but nobody paid any attention to her. "Stop telling us what to do," they shouted, when she tried to speak. And then everyone laughed.

Jimmy was so pleased. It had been a nightmare, a real nightmare – which actually it had been, because he now woke up. He had been dreaming about football being banned – such a silly dream – and now he was wide awake and had to get up and go off to a football match with his father.

"I had a very strange dream last night," he said to his father, as they drove down the road to the football ground.

"Oh yes," said his father. "What was it about?"

Jimmy thought for a moment. It was such a silly dream and it would take a long time to tell his father about it. So he simply said, "Freedom."

And that, he thought, was enough.

**More books by Alexander McCall Smith for 8-10-year olds, available from all good bookshops:**

| | |
|---|---|
| Akimbo and the Crocodile Man | ISBN: 978-1405218139 |
| Akimbo and the Elephants | ISBN: 978-1405218115 |
| Akimbo and the Lions | ISBN: 978-1405218122 |
| Akimbo and the Snakes | ISBN: 978-0747586234 |

**Find out more about Alexander McCall Smith and view a complete list of his children's books at www.braw.org.uk.**

# Lucky

a story for 10-14-year-olds

by
Catherine MacPhail

# Lucky

Last day of term, 7 weeks away from St Ambrose's High, I should have been over the moon, yet I was miserable.

We were in assembly and the Head Teacher, McDuff, was twittering away like a demented bird. He wanted us to pray to St Ambrose for a new school. He was always praying for a new school. Nobody ever listens to him. Certainly not St Ambrose.

I don't think McDuff's ever been right since the roof of the canteen fell on him. Bits of roof are always falling down in this old school. But I ended up getting the blame. And it wasn't my fault. I was only juggling a couple of rolls and they must have hit a weak bit in the ceiling. Just shows how hard the rolls were as well.

I got the blame anyway.

I always get the blame.

My pal, Ash, was in a great mood. "This time tomorrow, Dannyboy, I'll be on my way to sunny Pakistan," he said in his cheery voice.

I told him to shut up about sunny Pakistan but nothing shuts up the wee man.

My eyes were searching for one person. Karen Leslie. Girl of my dreams. The reason why I was so miserable. I wouldn't see her for 7 weeks either. She was at the other end of the hall, slouching in that dead cool way of hers, chewing gum, shirt open at the neck, tie at half-mast, her jet black hair standing out in spikes. She looked like a Goth version of the Statue of Liberty. Karen had big black eyes and legs that went right up to her chin. I'd always fancied her, but she never gave me a second glance. Come to that, she never gave me a first glance either. She was always surrounded by all the cool guys in the school...and I wasn't one of them.

And then, something happened that changed everything.

Ash was fiddling about with his mobile phone. I thought he was looking for the weather forecast for sunny Pakistan. But he wasn't. He was looking at the lottery numbers.

25, 15, 6, 8, 31...

The numbers rang a bell.

It was like a bulb being switched on in my head. Hadn't my mother bought a lottery ticket last Saturday, and those were her numbers? I remembered because she'd picked all the family's birthdays. Then, she'd stuck the ticket in my pocket and forgot all about it. It was still there, crumpled, wrapped round a bit of gum.

25, 15, 6, 8, 31...

I began to sweat. Had I seen right? I snatched the phone from Ash.

"What's wrong with you, Dannyboy?"

My imagination was working at warp speed.

I could be a millionaire.

Karen would never be able to resist a millionaire.

I could be cool. Get a makeover. Plastic surgery even.

Already I could picture me and Karen slouching into the sunset together.

I was just about to check that last number, lurking beneath the chewing gum, when I was grabbed by the tie and hauled out of the line.

"What are you doing with a mobile phone?" It was Mr Motivator, the PE teacher. He'd had it in for me since I'd stapled his shorts to the canteen wall. Man cannot take a joke. At least he wasn't wearing them at the time.

I tried to answer, but it's hard to talk when strangulation's setting in.

## Lucky

"Nothing to say, eh? Give me that!"

He grabbed the phone. Unfortunately, the lottery ticket stuck to his fingers as well.

He shook his hand to get free of it and it flew half way up the hall. I wasn't letting that ticket out of my sight. I dived, knocking down 3 other boys in the process. Somebody kicked the ticket. I rolled after it. Honest, a move worthy of James Bond. Boys went down like pins in a bowling alley.

McDuff didn't even notice. Still twittering on about St Ambrose.

By this time, Mr Motivator had called for backup. Two other teachers were after me now. Nothing was going to stop me getting that ticket.

I was flat on the floor, just about to reach for it. It was within my grasp, when my ankles were gripped and I was dragged back along the floor, watching the ticket disappear between a forest of legs.

Giving up was not an option.

I saw the ticket being lifted by the jannie, Big Rab. He's always cleaning up before you get a chance to dirty anything.

With a yell, I yanked myself free, and I was off. I skited out of the hall, Mr Motivator and his gang only steps behind me.

Big Rab was already striding down the corridor, his bin clutched in his arms.

With a spurt of speed I raced past him, snatching the bin out of his hands as I did. A hanging offence in Rab's eyes. His bins are sacred.

"Give me that back, boy!"

And before I knew it he was after me too.

As I ran, my hand was searching that bin. Disgusting the things that were in there. A banana skin. I threw it behind me and heard Big Rab squeal as he went flying on it. One down.

A polystyrene box filled with chips was next. It was in the air and hit Mr Motivator square in the face, tomato sauce went everywhere.

I plucked out my ticket, and chucked the bin away. I heard it roll and the other 2 teachers tumbled over it.

I had beaten them all!

I slid round a corner, and smacked right into McDuff's life-sized statue of St Ambrose. St Ambrose swayed. He shook. The candles around him flickered. I threw my arms up. Tried to stop him falling. But he was too big for me. Down he went, hitting the ground face first. The candles rolled across the floor.

I had committed the worst sin. I had broken St Ambrose. Now I really was for it.

But I had my ticket. And when I explained to McDuff, he would understand. I mean, I would buy him a statue of St Ambrose for every classroom. I'd even build him a new school.

But for the moment, I'd hide in a cupboard.

I must have been there 10 minutes when the alarm went off.

Fire drill, today of all days.

However, as I made my way out of the school, I noticed a definite air of panic. Somewhere in the distance I could hear a fire engine.

Blinking hell, this wasn't a drill.

The school was on fire.

Outside, teachers were running wild checking to make sure we were all accounted for. Pupils were cheering.

It was an old school, falling to bits anyway. It didn't take long for the fire to take hold.

I found Ash, watching in amazement.

"Dreams do come true, Dannyboy," he said.

I handed him the ticket. "Check that for me. I think I'm a millionaire."

Mr Motivator caught sight of me. "If I find out you had anything to do with this, boy..."

Oh no, they weren't going to park the blame for this on me. "It wasnae me, sir. Honest!"

"You haven't heard the last of this!" he roared, then he was gone.

Ash pulled me round. "Did you start the fire?"

He didn't wait for an answer. He was suddenly shouting at the top of his voice. "Hey, Dannyboy here started the fire."

Why did I always get the blame? I had nothing to do with this...

Did I?

I tried to push the memory of St Ambrose and his holy candles out of my mind. Could still picture them rolling towards the billowing curtains at the windows.

No. A few wee holy candles couldn't have done this much damage...surely?

The school was going wild. The word was getting passed across the playground.

"Dannyboy burnt the school doon."

And then, as if by magic, Karen was at my side. "You burnt the school doon? That's pretty cool."

I was ready to protest my innocence. Honest, I was, but Karen was staring at me with those huge panda eyes, blowing a big pink bubble right in my face. She looked well impressed.

Just then McDuff came hurrying out of the school. He had rescued the statue of St Ambrose and had it tucked under his arm. His nose was missing, (St Ambrose's, not McDuff's). It must have come off when he fell.

And it suddenly came to me, this is just what McDuff had been praying for. He would get his new school now. Me and St Ambrose had answered his prayers.

Ash broke into my thoughts. "You're a nutjob, Dannyboy." He handed me my ticket. "This is for 2 weeks ago. After all that you didn't win a thing."

I looked at Karen. Flames were reflected in her black eyes as if they were on fire. And I knew I had won something.

I caught sight of St Ambrose again, and you can say it was a trick of the light, but I'm sure he winked at me.

**The first 2 books in Catherine MacPhail's gripping new series, *Nemesis*, published by Bloomsbury Children's Books, are now available from all good bookshops:**

Nemesis: Into the Shadows  ISBN: 978-0747582687

Nemesis: The Beast Within  ISBN: 978-0747582694

**Find out more about Catherine MacPhail and her books at www.braw.org.uk.**

## More About Scottish Book Trust

Scottish Book Trust is Scotland's national agency for reading and writing. We are a unique organisation committed to the promotion of reading and books. We believe in the value of making every child a reading child, every adult a reading adult, and every reader a lover of good books. Books expand intellectual, emotional and imaginative horizons, enriching people's lives and experiences.

www.scottishbooktrust.com

## The Scottish Book Trust Children's Programme

Scottish Book Trust has a packed children's programme for young people of all ages, including:

- **www.braw.org.uk**
  For loads of information about your favourite Scottish children's authors and illustrators, an online children's bookclub, games, puzzles and lots more, log on to www.braw.org.uk.

# More About Scottish Book Trust

- **Scottish Friendly National Words on Wheels Touring Programme**
  A unique touring programme taking national and international children's authors to schools and public venues right across Scotland, from Skye to Shetland, from Glasgow to Inverness, talking to audiences of 4 to over 1,000.

- **Royal Mail Awards for Scottish Children's Books**
  Scotland's biggest book award voted for by thousands of children and young people across the country. Log on to www.braw.org.uk/royalmailawards to get involved.

- **On the Money**
  An innovative new initiative to publish Scottish children's stories to educate and inform children's attitudes to money, sponsored by Standard Life Bank in association with Learning and Teaching Scotland. Find out more at www.ltscotland.org.uk/onthemoney.

- **Author and Illustrator Visits**
  Over 1,200 author and illustrator visits to schools, libraries and communities the length and breadth of Scotland part-funded by Scottish Book Trust every year.

**For more information on any of the above, visit www.scottishbooktrust.com**

**Scottish Book Trust is a registered charity and receives foundation funding from the Scottish Arts Council.**

# Further Resources

There are a huge number of talented authors and illustrators for children and young adults living and working in Scotland. Here are a few places where you can find out more about them and their work:

## www.braw.org.uk

Log on for a comprehensive list of authors and illustrators resident in Scotland together with a complete directory of their books.

## www.BooksfromScotland.com

An online bookshop selling the widest possible range of Scottish books and authors, providing customers with the latest information on what's new and hot in Scottish writing, including a large selection of children's books.

### Reading Round Edinburgh:
### A Guide to Children's Books of the City
### with an introduction by J.K. Rowling

From its secret underground streets to the top of Arthur's Seat, the city of Edinburgh has been the inspiration for many children's books and writers. This unique guide will help children and adults to discover Edinburgh through its children's books – and to discover new books and writers through their city. With full-colour, child-friendly maps for different areas of Edinburgh, the book can be used as an informative walking guide around Edinburgh, or read as a fascinating overview of the city's rich contribution to children's literature. The contributors to the book represent the cream of Edinburgh children's writing, from Joan Lingard and Mollie Hunter to Keith Gray, Gill Arbuthnott and Nicola Morgan. Available from Floris Books: www.florisbooks.co.uk